A Hawai'i Cinderella Story

Sumorella

Sandi Takayama

Illustrated by Esther Szegedy

THE
BESS
PRESS

3565 Harding Ave. Honolulu, Hawai'i 96816

Once upon a time, on an island in the middle of the ocean, there lived a young boy, his mother and father, and his two older brothers. They lived in an old house in the middle of a huge yard, surrounded by mango trees.

Each morning the boy's mother and father went off to the little corner market where they sold their mango specialties. People came from all over the island to buy their delicious mango bread, mango chutney, mango seed, and, of course, pickled mango.

Each afternoon his two older brothers went off to sumo practice at the neighborhood park. And each day after school the young boy was left to do all the chores.

He picked the mangoes, peeled, sliced, and chopped them. He trimmed the tree branches, raked up the leaves, and threw away all the (ugh!) rotten mangoes. Everyone called him Mango Boy.

The day came for the local sumo exhibition. Rumor had it that a famous stablemaster from Japan was visiting the islands in hopes of recruiting some local talent. The two older brothers were competing in the exhibition, but when the young boy begged to go with them they just laughed.

"What? Mango Boy, you like go wit' us? No way! You so shrimpy da mawashi not going even stay on. Go gain one noddah two, t'ree hundred pounds, all right!"

And they cracked up all the way to the park.

Mango Boy wished more than
anything that he could compete
in the exhibition. "But how I can go?
No mo' time. Always get so much work
fo' do." He sighed as he sat down under a mango tree.
Just then Mango Boy's good friend, the manapua man, came
strolling down the lane calling out, "Hot manapua! Hot manapua!"
When he reached the house he lifted the bamboo pole off his
shoulders and looked closely at Mango Boy.
"Eh, you all right or what, boy? You look funny kine."
Mango Boy shook his head. "Nah, nothing. Just t'inking." He looked
around, then whispered to the manapua man,
"No tell nobody, but I like be in da sumo stuff today."

"You? You like be one sumotori?"

"I know, I know. I stay small,
but I pretty fast, you know.
I practice my moves morning
time before everybody get up.
I just need one chance
to prove myself."

The manapua man shrugged.
"Sounds pupule to me,
but, ah, go den, go den.
I go do your work fo' you."

"What? Nah, I no can ask you fo' do 'em all by yourself."

"Eh, I stay old, but I can handle. Dis your chance. Bettah go fo' it!"

Mango Boy didn't move. "But I no mo' one mawashi and I don't know how make my hair nice kine way."

"No worry, no worry," said the manapua man with a smile. "Just bring me one pumpkin, some mice and one big rat."

Mango Boy quickly gathered everything.

The manapua man took a bite out of one of the manapuas and waved it in the air. The next instant Mango Boy was standing next to a golden coach complete with horses and coachmen. He was dressed in a satin ball gown with the daintiest glass slippers on his feet.

The manapua man jumped back in surprise. "Wow! Sorry, boy, I wen' make you get da wrong t'ings. Hoo, let me t'ink now. Sumotori, sumotori. Oh yeah, yeah, I t'ink you gotta get five bags poi, two pots rice, and, uh, twelve green bananas. I t'ink dat's it."

Mango Boy took quite a while
gathering up the items.
(It was difficult getting around in the
ball gown and glass slippers.)
Finally, he placed everything in front
of the manapua man. The manapua
man looked it over and said,
"Okay, now you gotta eat 'um."

"What?" yelled Mango Boy. "I gotta eat all dat?"

"Yeah, why?" replied the manapua man. "What you t'ink? Sumotori just drink water all day?"

Mango Boy smiled weakly and started to dig in. He managed to eat one and a half bags of poi, three cups of rice, and seven green bananas before collapsing on the ground with a huge burp.

Again the manapua man took a bite of the manapua, waved it in the air, and suddenly Mango Boy stood dressed in a mawashi made of the most beautiful silk brocade. His hair gleamed in an elaborate topknot. The manapua man walked around looking at him. "You stay little bit mo' tall, but still way too skinny. No can help though, you nevah eat all da stuff, dat's why."

"I no care," said Mango Boy.

"Good enough, good enough. T'anks, eh!"

As Mango Boy turned to run to the
exhibition, the manapua man yelled,
"Oh, yeah, I almos' wen' forget.
From now on you Sumorella,
not Mango Boy,
and no forget come back by kau-kau time
or your mawashi going fall
right off your 'ōkole."

Sumorella made it just in time. When he first took his place on the dohyo, the crowd roared with laughter. But as the exhibition went on and he continued to beat each of his opponents, the laughter turned to cheers. "Sumorella, Sumorella!" they chanted.

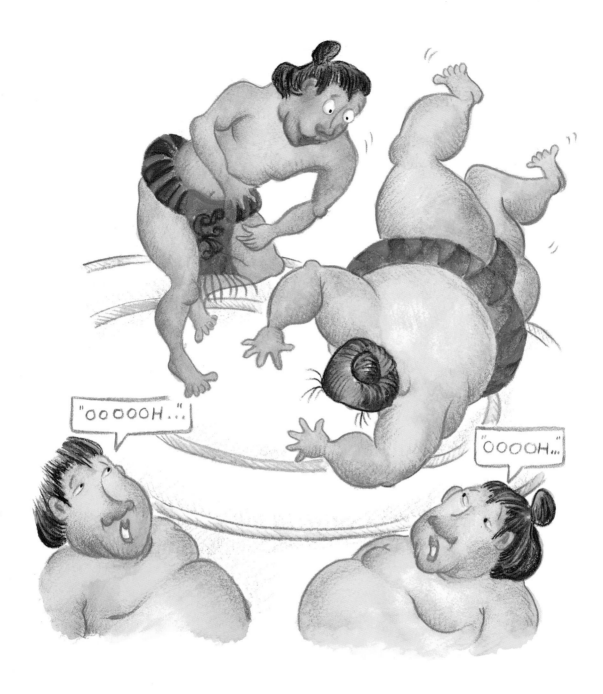

Soon it was time for the final match. Sumorella's stomach began to growl as he grappled with the opponent, and he realized with alarm that it was almost kau-kau time. With one last heave he threw his opponent out of the dohyo.

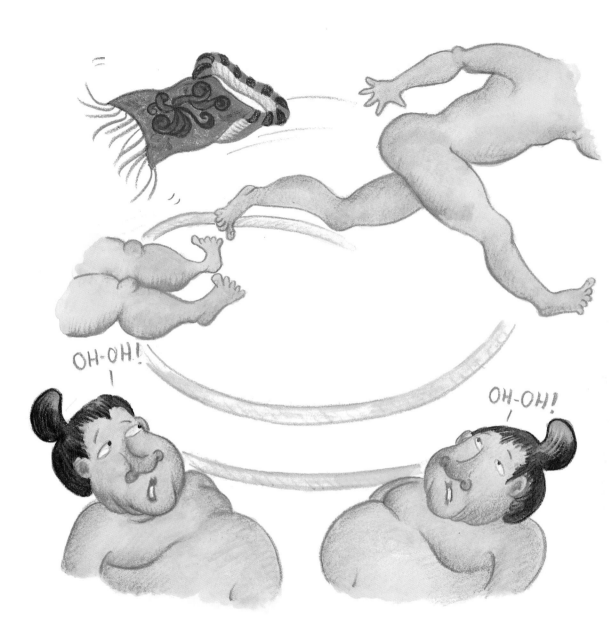

His mawashi fell off, but he kept on running. He escaped through the nearest exit. When he reached home, he was himself again.

Sumorella glanced around. All the chores were done
and the manapua man was just slipping the bamboo pole
back onto his shoulders. Before Sumorella could say a word,
the manapua man flashed a shaka sign
and disappeared
down the lane.

At dinner that night his brothers could only exclaim about the skinny sumotori who had won every match and then vanished mysteriously, leaving nothing behind but his mawashi. The stablemaster was going from house to house looking for the sumotori who could fit into it.

When the stablemaster arrived, the brothers tried every trick they knew to squeeze into the mawashi. They grunted and groaned, pulled and tugged, but they could barely get a leg in it.

The stablemaster was about
to leave when he noticed Sumorella sitting in the mango tree.
He bowed politely and said, "Gomen nasai, perhaps you like to try on
mawashi, too?"

"Ah, no bother wit' him," laughed his brothers, "unless you like him
wrestle one mango or somet'ing." But the stablemaster insisted.

Sumorella climbed down from the tree. He tried on the mawashi, and to everyone's surprise, it fit perfectly! The stablemaster immediately invited Sumorella to come live in Japan and train at the finest sumo stable there.

Sumorella worked hard and eventually reached the rank of yokozuna. He became one of the most famous sumotori in Japan and was well loved by people everywhere. When he retired from sumo he returned home and married a former Miss Hawai'i. He later became a trustee for one of the wealthiest private estates in the islands. And for the rest of his life he never ever had to pick up a rotten mango again.

Glossary

dohyo	sumo ring
Gomen nasai	Japanese for "Excuse me."
kau-kau	slang for food, a meal
manapua	Hawaiian name for a dumpling filled with pork or bean paste
mango	yellowish red fruit with a firm skin and juicy, sweet-smelling pulp
mawashi	belt worn by sumotori, made of cotton or silk. Except in fairy tales, the fancy kesho mawashi, or ceremonial apron, worn by Sumorella and his opponent, is not worn during the match.
'ōkole	slang for buttocks
poi	Hawaiian food made from steamed taro root pounded into a paste
pupule	Hawaiian word meaning "crazy"
shaka	hand signal made by curling the middle three fingers and extending the thumb and little finger. It is used as a friendly greeting.
sumo	Japanese sport in which two men compete against each other inside a clay ring. The first to step outside the ring or touch the ring floor with any part of his body except his feet loses the match.
sumotori	man who competes in a sumo match
yokozuna	highest rank in sumo